Dream songs 🦟 Night songs

FROM MALI TO LOUISIANA

Around the world, the children sleep. Around the world, stars twinkle beside the smiling moon. A través del mundo, los niños duermen. A través del mundo, las estrellas brillan y a su lado la luna sonríe. Partout dans le monde, les enfants sommeillent. Partout dans le monde, les étoiles brillent et la lune sourit.

It's time for dinner now
Es la hora de comer
C'est maintenant l'heure du souper
MALI

Tomorrow, we shall begin our journey
Mañana, comenzaremos un viaje
Demain, nous partirons en voyage
EASTERN EUROPE

And cross the ocean at rest
Juntos, atravesaremos un mar tranquilo
Nous traverserons la mer qui se repose

AUSTRALIA

To discover lands unknown
Descubriremos tierras desconocidas
Vers une terre inconnue

JAPAN

For now, we must sleep
Ahora, durmamos
Maintenant, dormons
TCHAD

And dream happy thoughts
Soñemos en los buenos momentos que nos esperan
Rêvons au bon temps devant nous
LOUISIANA

Sing joy to the world
Cantemos juntos al mundo
Célébrons la terre
CANADA (HURON-WENDAT)

Invent new stories
Inventemos nuevas historias
Inventons des histoires
POLAND

The stars will show us the way
Una estrella brillante nos guiará
Une belle étoile nous guidera
SOUTH AFRICA

The moon's light will fall on our path
La luna mostrara el camino
La lune annoncera le chemin
ITALY

New friends will come along
Haremos nuevos amigos
On se fera de nouveaux amis
COSTA RICA

We'll share our memories
Compartamos nuestros recuerdos
Nous partagerons nos souvenirs

ARMENIA

And there will be music

Y habrá música
Et il y aura de la musique
SPAIN

Tomorrow, we shall begin our journey
Mañana, continuaremos nuestro viaje
Demain, nous partirons en voyage
CANADA

Record Producer Paul Campagne Artistic Director Roland Stringer Recorded by Paul Campagne and Davy Gallant at Studio King and Dogger Pond Studio Mixed by Davy Gallant at Dogger Pond Studio Mastering Renée Marc-Aurèle at SNB Illustrations Sylvie Bourbonnière Story Patrick Lacoursière Spanish translation Guillermo Jareda Design Stephan Lorti for Haus Design Communications

SINGERS H'Sao (Caleb Rimtobaye, Israël Rimtobaye, Amos Rimtobaye, Service Ledjebgue, Dono Bei Ledjebgue et Taroum Rimtobaye) Makun, Thula Thula, Kondo Sylva Balassanian Yeraz Mary Burke Owaiyare Paul Campagne Little fishy, Owaiyare, Dodo bébé Michelle Campagne Chanson gitane, Owaiyare, Dodo bébé, Na wojtusia z popielnika, Thula Thula, Je te dis merci Suzanne Campagne Makun, Dodo bébé, Durme hermosa donzella, La ninna nanna del cavallino Juan Jose Carranza Los pollitos dicen Paul Kunigis Na wojtusia z popielnika Nathalie Picard Sadraskwiio MUSICIANS Paul Campagne classic and acoustic guitar, kalimba, bongos, shakers, bass, accordion Michel Dupire djembe, dijeridoo berumbau, pandero, percussions, gong, chimes, talking drum, shaker, castanets Bob Cohen mandolin cello, guitaret Jonathan Moorman violin Davy Gallant mandolin (Na wojtusia z popielnika, Je te dis merci), acoustic guitar (Je te dis merci) Luc Lopez accordion (Na wojtusia z popielnika) Michelle Campagne accordion (La ninna nanna del cavallino), piano (Je te dis merci) Michel Dubeau duduk (Yeraz), flute (Owaiyare) Guy Bell oud (Yeraz) Juan Jose Carranza flamenco guitar (Durme hemosa donzella) bongos, shaker (Los pollitos dicen) Caleb Rimtobaye classical guitar (Kondo) Natalie Picard drum, flute, voix (Sadraskwiio) MUSICAL ARRANGEMENTS All songs by Paul Campagne except Sadraskwiio (Nathalie Picard), Na wojtusia z popielnika (Paul Kunigis), Los pollitos dicen (Juan Jose Carranza), Yeraz (Sylva Balassanian), Kalon (Caleb Rimtobaye), Dodo bébé and Je te dis merci (Michelle Campagne).

THANKS TO Michel Cusson, François Asselin, Mona Cochingyan, Isabelle Desaulniers, Patricia Huot, Véronique Croisile, Dominique Villa, Connie Kaldor, Stephan Lorti, Patrick Sirois, Natalie Bergeron, Dan Behrman, Paul Etch, Gina Brault, Marc Labelle, Jacques Maltais, Hiroya Miura, Yoko Sayeki, Janet Lumb, Bénédicte Froissart.

WWW.THESECRETMOUNTAIN.COM ISBN 2-923163-06-0 2003 Ⓟ Folle Avoine Productions Ⓒ Homestead Music